# Disney

# Aladdin

By Anne Lynn
Illustrated by the DRI Artworks

*Once upon a time in a land called Agrabah lived the beautiful and clever Princess Jasmine. The Sultan's laws stated that the princess had to marry a prince by her next birthday, and time was running out. . . .*

"Jasmine, it's the law!" the Sultan insisted. "It will be your birthday in just three days!"

"I don't love Prince Achmed!" Jasmine replied. "Oh, Father, how can you force me to marry someone I don't love?"

4

Jasmine held back her tears as her father left the palace garden.

"Oh, Rajah!" she said to her pet tiger. "Whatever will I do?" She looked up at the high wall surrounding the palace. If she could just climb over that wall, she would be free!

So, that night, Jasmine disguised herself. Rajah was sad to see Jasmine leave, but he still helped his friend escape.

Once over the palace wall, Jasmine suddenly found herself alone in a world she had never before experienced— Agrabah's bustling marketplace.

Seeing a hungry child, she took an apple from a fruit stand and gave it to him.

"You'd better pay for that, you little street urchin!" yelled the fruit seller.

"P-pay?" Jasmine stammered. "B-but I have no money!"

Suddenly, a young man emerged from the crowd and rescued the princess. He told her his name was Aladdin.

Aladdin grabbed Jasmine's hand and took her to a rooftop far above the streets. "We'll be safe here," he said. "Where do you come from?"

"I ran away from home," Jasmine replied. "My father is trying to force me to get married!"

"That's awful," Aladdin said.

Just then, the palace guards burst into Aladdin's hiding place. Before Aladdin could get away, he was taken prisoner.

Jasmine threw back her hood. "Release him at once!" she ordered.

"Princess Jasmine!" the palace guard said with a gasp.

"Princess?" said the surprised Aladdin.

"I dare not release him," said the captain of the guards. "My orders come from Jafar. You will have to take it up with him."

"Believe me, I will!" Jasmine said.

Back at the palace, Jasmine confronted her father's chief adviser, Jafar.

"I command you to release Aladdin!" said the angry princess.

"But, Princess, Aladdin has already been executed!" Jafar lied.

Jasmine gasped. "When I marry and become queen, you'll pay for this, Jafar!" she cried, running from the room.

That evening, Jafar disguised himself as an old man and slipped quietly into the dungeon where Aladdin was being held.

"You don't always have to be poor," the disguised Jafar said to Aladdin and his pet monkey, Abu. "There is a cave filled with treasure! It can be yours if you will just help me get a worthless lamp."

Eager to get out of the dungeon, Aladdin agreed to help the old man.

So, Aladdin, Abu, and Jafar set off into the desert. When they got to the cave, Aladdin and Abu entered quickly.

Inside the cave among piles of treasure, they found a Magic Carpet and the lamp. They grabbed both and headed back to Jafar. As they reached the cave entrance, the ground began to shake violently. Jafar grabbed the lamp from Aladdin. As he did, Abu bit him on the hand. Then Abu, Aladdin, and the lamp fell back into the cave.

"We're trapped in here, Abu!" Aladdin said, rubbing the dusty lamp.

The lamp began to glow. Then a cloud of smoke poured out from the spout and formed itself into a gigantic genie!

"If you're a real genie, you could get us out of this cave!" Aladdin said.

Quick as a wink, the three were soaring over the desert on the Magic Carpet.

The Genie told Aladdin he could make a wish.

"I wish . . . I wish to be a prince!"

The next day, the palace gates were thrown open.

"Prince Ali of Ababwa!" announced a palace guard. Trumpets blared. Drums rolled. And into the palace came . . . Aladdin on the Magic Carpet!

He was dressed from turban to toe in the silks and jewels of a royal prince.

"Your Majesty, I have journeyed from afar to seek your daughter's hand in marriage," he said to the astonished Sultan.

That night, Prince Ali took Jasmine for a moonlight ride on the Magic Carpet. She soon discovered that he was the same young man she had met in the marketplace.

Far below, Jafar watched them. "I must get rid of that intruder before he spoils my plans to marry the princess!" he said.

When Jasmine and Aladdin returned to the palace, the princess rushed off to talk to her father.

At once, Jafar's guards captured Aladdin. They carried him to a high cliff and pushed him into the sea below. Luckily, he still had the lamp. Nearly unconscious, he rubbed it and made a wish.

Meanwhile, Jasmine found her father in the courtyard. "I want to marry Prince Ali," she said.

But Jafar interrupted. "I'm afraid that's impossible, Princess! Prince Ali has . . . gone away."

Then, Jafar held his cobra-headed staff before the Sultan's eyes. The snake's eyes began to glow.

"You will marry Jafar," the hypnotized Sultan droned.

"Never!" Jasmine cried. "Father! What's wrong with you?"

"I know," said a voice.

It was Aladdin! He threw the cobra staff to the floor. It shattered into pieces.

"Jafar, you are eternally banned from my kingdom!" the Sultan said.

The next day, the Sultan announced, "From this day forth, the princess shall marry whomever she deems worthy!"

"I choose you, Aladdin!" Jasmine cried.

Then they married and lived happily ever after.